Boo to you, Piglittle

Sally Grindley • Andy Ellis

Gertie Goat came to visit her friend
Primrose Pig and all her piglets.
"Look at my beautiful sugarplums,"
Primrose Pig said proudly.

"He's got a cheeky little face!" said Gertie Goat, looking at Piglittle.

"Oh no," said Primrose Pig. "He's as good as gold."

But as soon as Primrose Pig turned her back, Piglittle slipped out of the sty and ran off.

First he ran into the henhouse.
"BOO!" he squeaked loudly.

"SHOO, SHOO!" squawked Hetty Hen.
"You've made me break one of my eggs."

Next he ran into the cowshed.
"BOO!" he squeaked loudly.

"MOO, MOO!" mooed Coral Cow. "You've made me spill my milk."

Then Piglittle ran to the sheep pens.
"BOO!" he squeaked loudly.

"BAA, BAA!" bleated Cheryl Sheep. "You've woken my lambs."

Who can I visit next?
wondered Piglittle.

He was just running past the
great big field, when Baggy Bull
bellowed for his supper.

Piglittle nearly jumped out of his skin.

He raced across the farmyard, into his sty and dived under Primrose.

"Where have you been, my sugarplum?" said Primrose Pig. "You must never run off without telling me. You could get hurt."